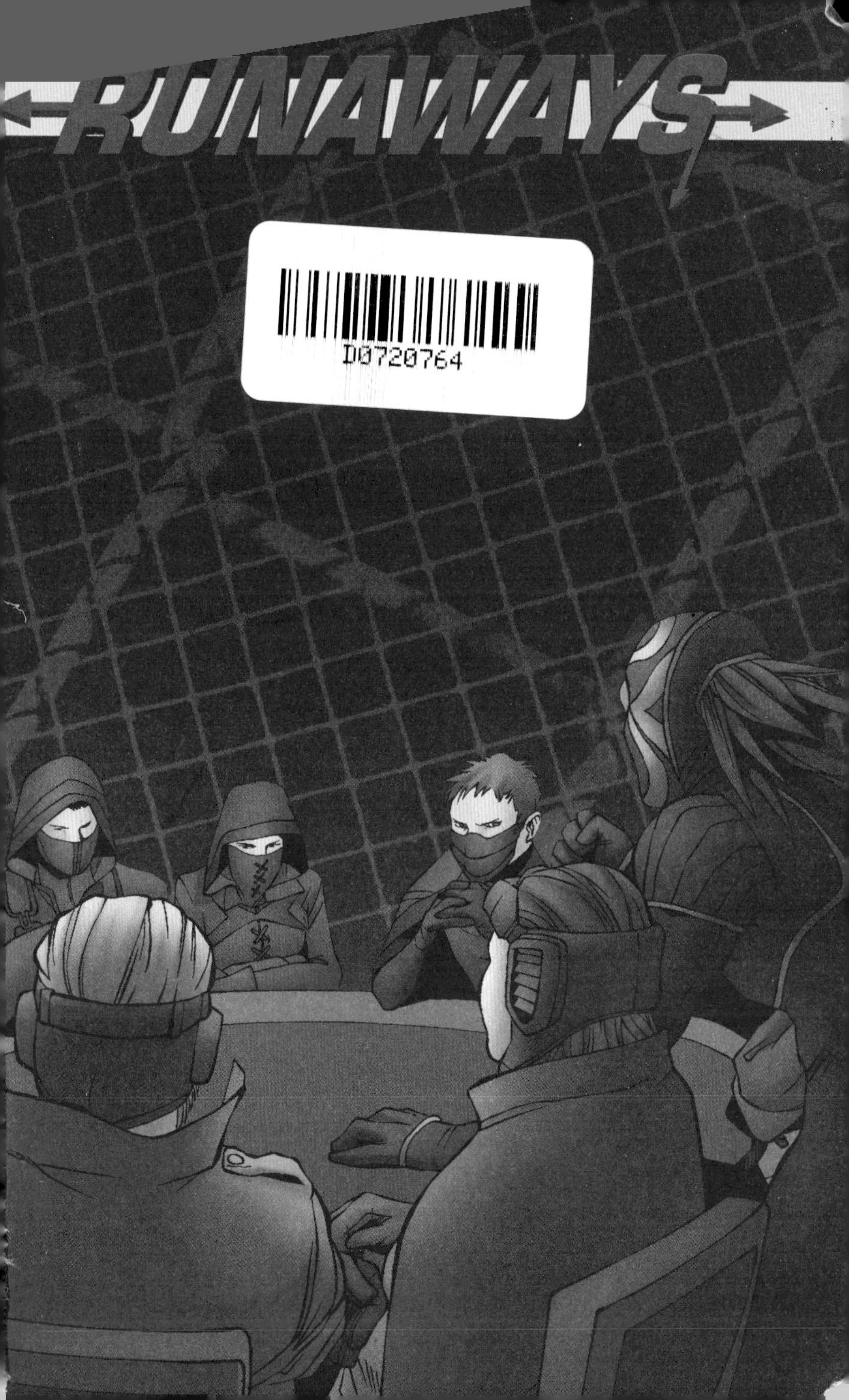
RUNAWAYS

PREVIOUSLY...

Teenager Alex Wilder and five other only children always thought that their parents were boring Los Angeles socialites, until the kids witness the adults murder a young girl in some kind of dark sacrificial ritual. The teens soon learn that their parents are part of a secret organization called The Pride, a collection of crime bosses, time-travelling despots, alien overlords, mad scientists, evil mutants and dark wizards.

After stealing weapons and resources from these villainous adults (including a mystical staff, futuristic gauntlets and a genetically engineered velociraptor named Old Lace), the kids run away from home and vow to bring their parents to justice. But when the members of The Pride frame their children for the murder they committed, the fugitive Runaways are forced to retreat to a subterranean hideout nicknamed the Hostel. Using the diverse powers and skills they inherited, the Runaways now hope to atone for their parents' crimes by helping those in need.

RUNAWAYS

TEENAGE WASTELAND

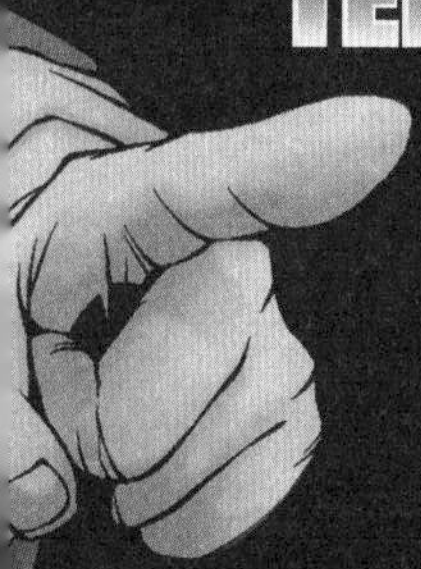

"Teenage Wasteland"

Writer: Brian K. Vaughan
Pencils: Adrian Alphona
Inks: Craig Yeung

"Lost and Found"

Writer: Brian K. Vaughan
Pencils: Takeshi Miyazawa
Inks: David Newbold

Colors: UDON's Christina Strain with Brian Reber
Letterer: Virtual Calligraphy's Randy Gentile
Cover Art: Jo Chen
Assistant Editor: MacKenzie Cadenhead
Editor: C.B. Cebulski

Collections Editor: Jeff Youngquist
Assistant Editor: Jennifer Grünwald
Book Designer: Carrie Beadle
Creative Director: Tom Marvelli

Editor in Chief: Joe Quesada
Publisher: Dan Buckley

RUNAWAYS created by
Brian K. Vaughan and Adrian Alphona

#7

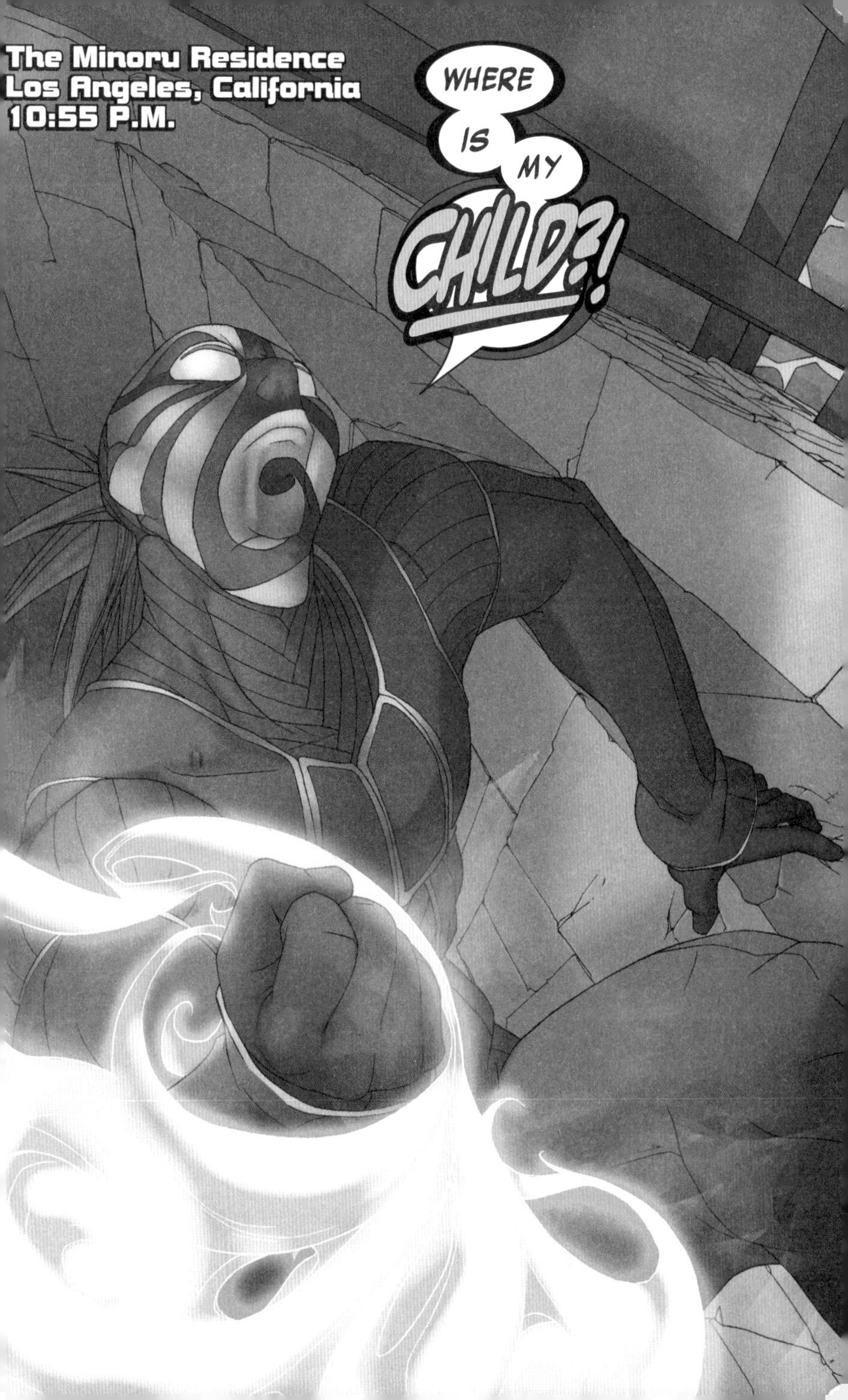
The Minoru Residence
Los Angeles, California
10:55 P.M.
WHERE IS MY CHILD?!

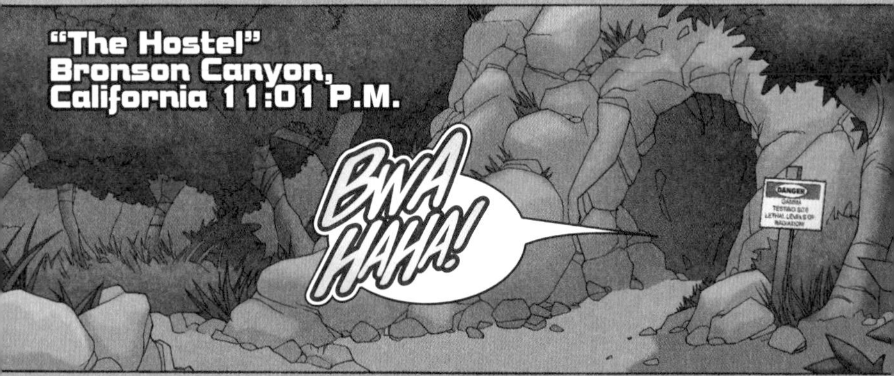
"The Hostel"
Bronson Canyon, California 11:01 P.M.
BWAHAHA!
DANGER

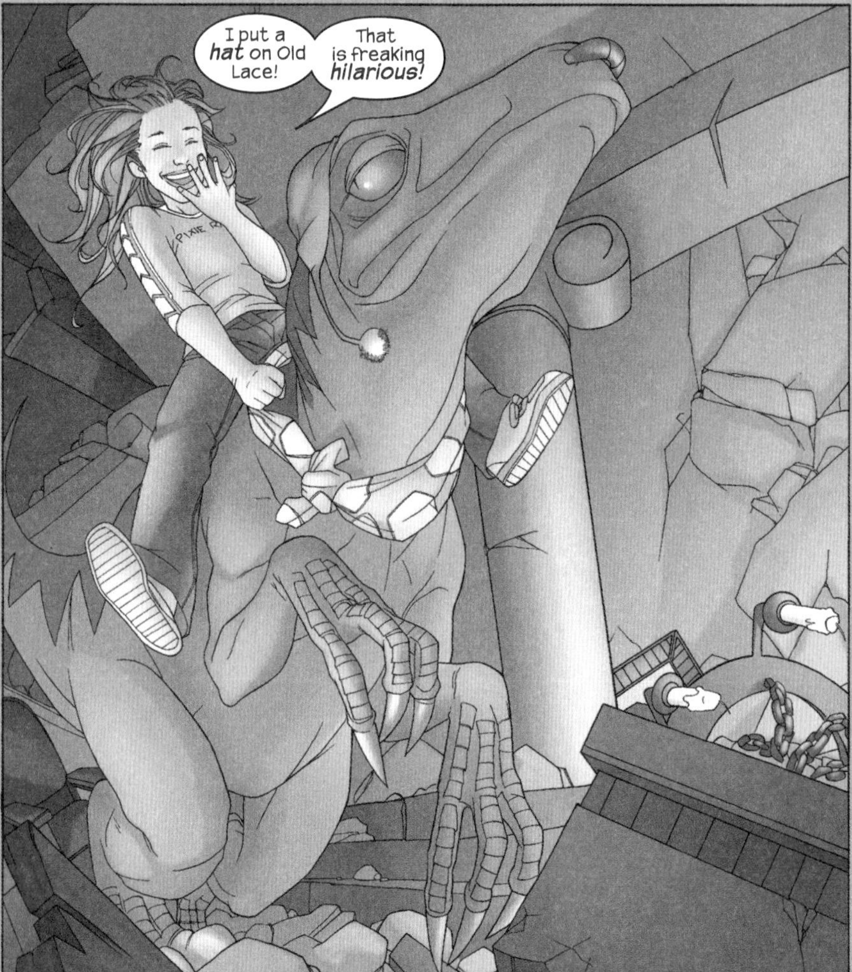
I put a hat on Old Lace!
That is freaking hilarious!

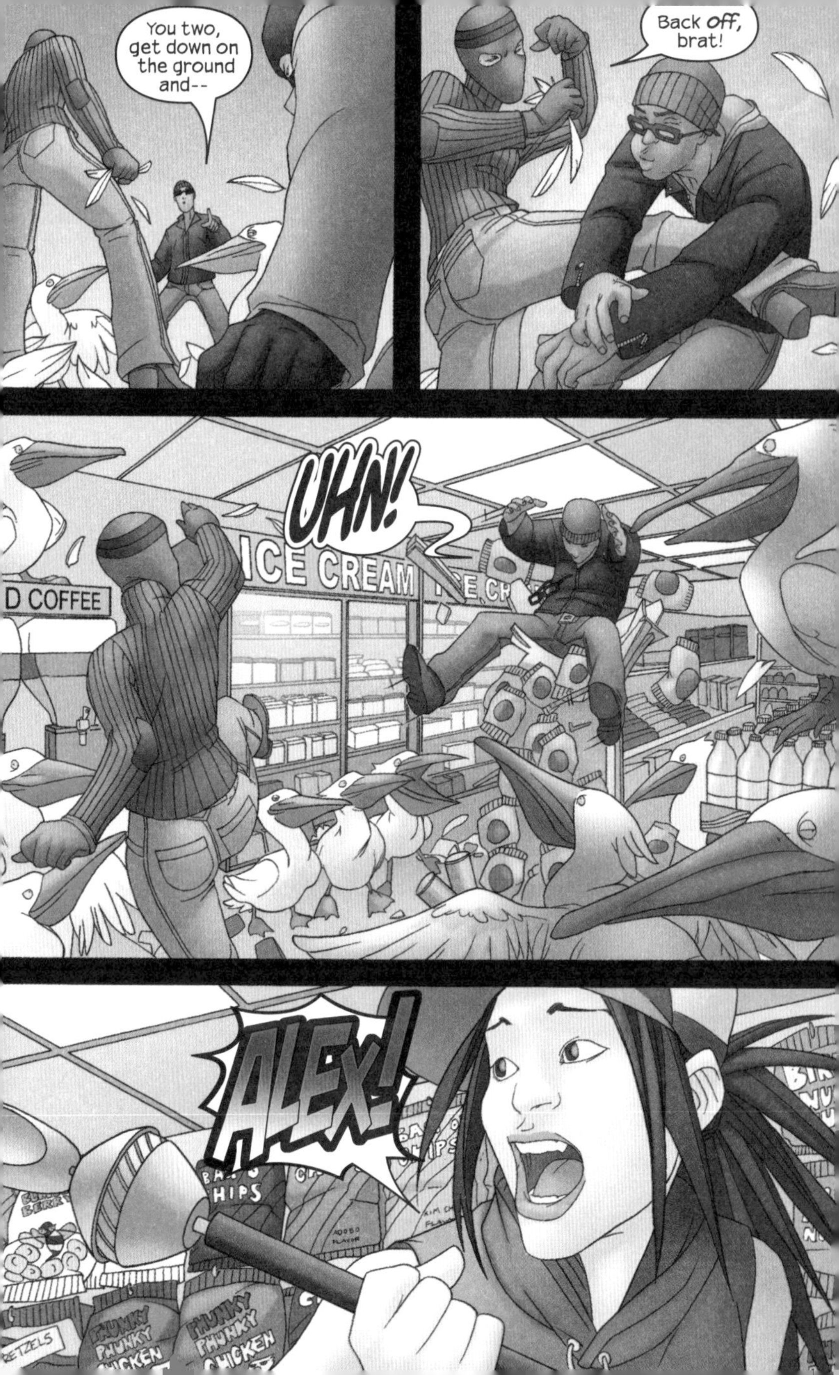
You two, get down on the ground and--
Back off, brat!
UHN!
ICE CREAM
D COFFEE
ALEX!
CHIPS
PHUNKY PHUNKY CHICKEN
PHUNKY PHUNKY CHICKEN
RETZELS

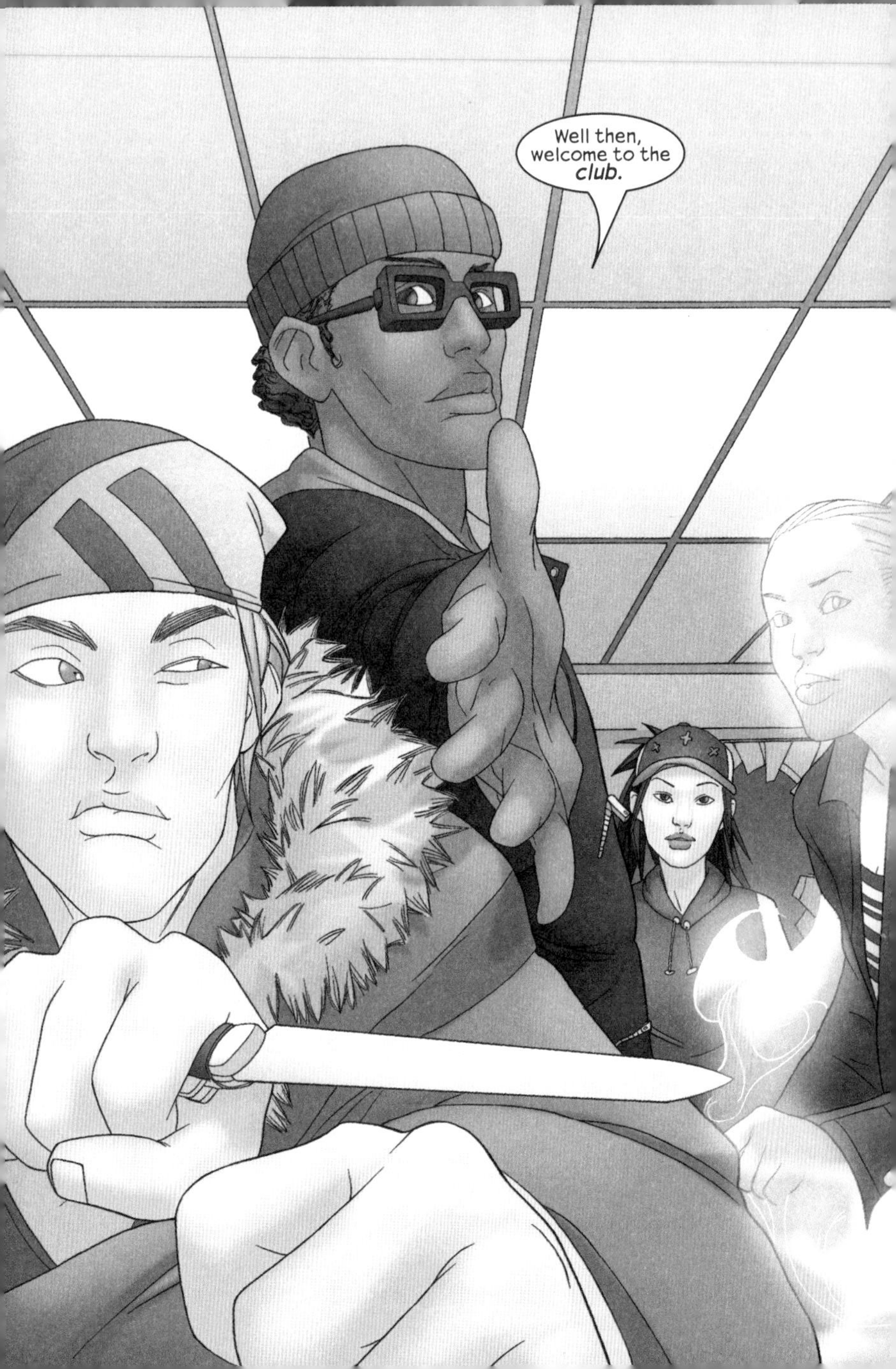
Well then, welcome to the *club.*

#8

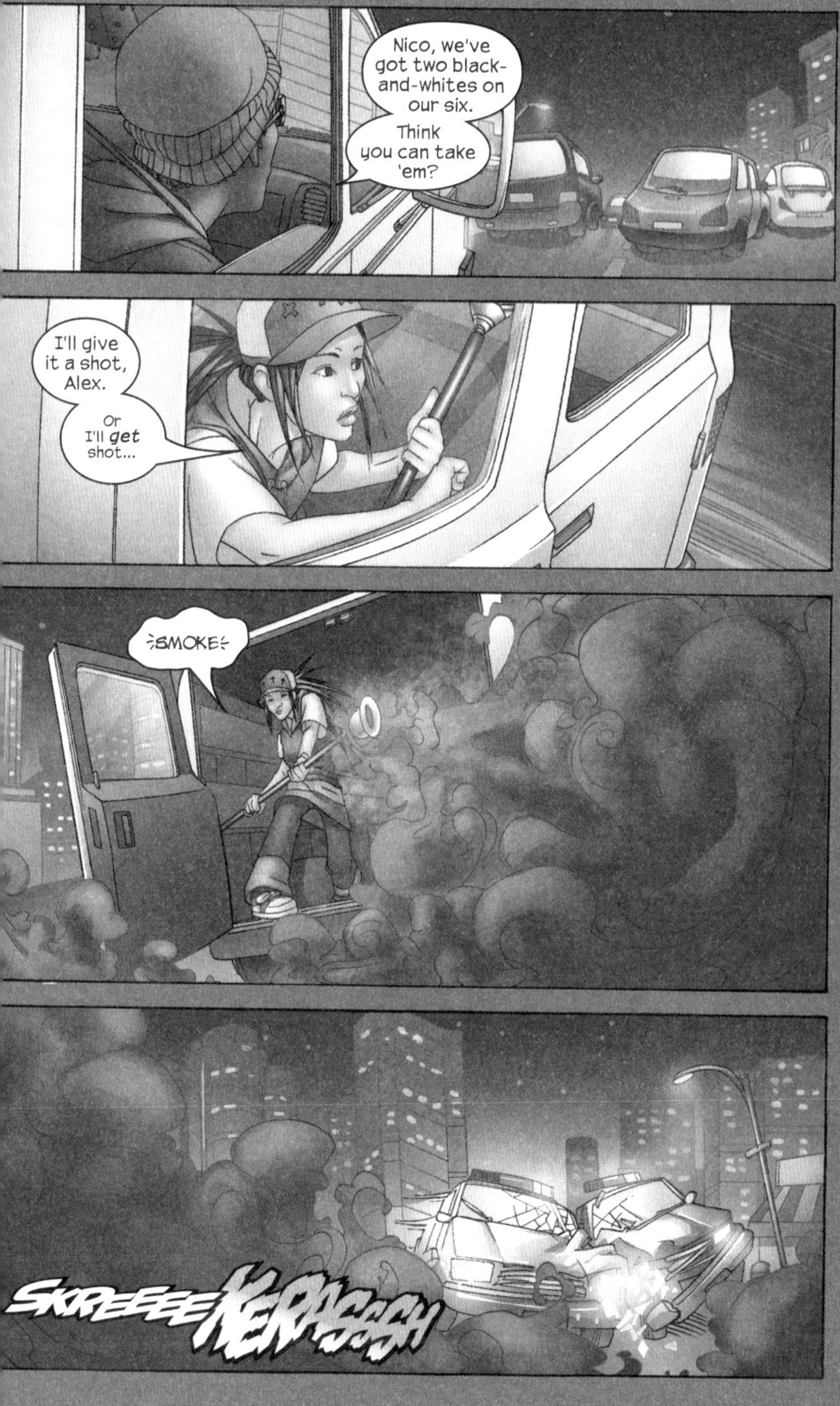
Nico, we've got two black-and-whites on our six.
Think you can take 'em?
I'll give it a shot, Alex.
Or I'll get shot...
SMOKE
SKREEEEE KERASSSH

Man, I don't know how you guys have adjusted so quickly to the fact that your parents are... you know.

It's like, growing up in Cali, you hear about *Doc Ock* and *Venom* and the *Punisher* and whatever on TV, but they always felt far away and... and *make-believe*.

We've had more time than you, Topher. It never really sinks in all the way, but it *will* start to feel like less of a bad dream.

Besides, unlike my folks, your mom and dad don't sound like they *chose* the path they're on. I'm sure we'll be able to get them some help. Set them straight again.

I hope so.

Ever since I was twelve, all I wanted was to get away from my stupid parents... and as soon as I get my wish, I just want everything back the way it was.

That's life, isn't it?

Yeah.

Yeah, I guess it is.

Topher, *wait.*

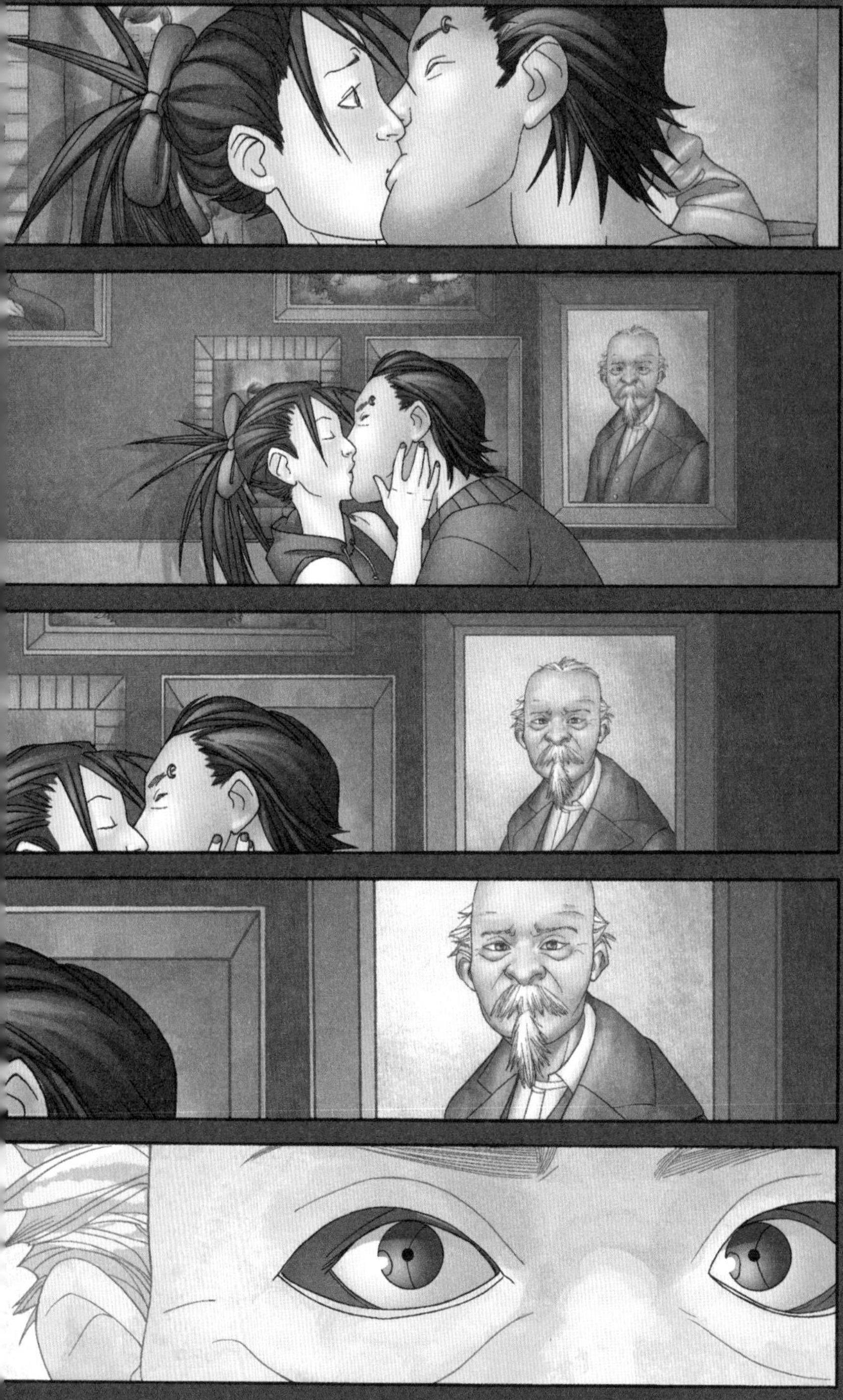

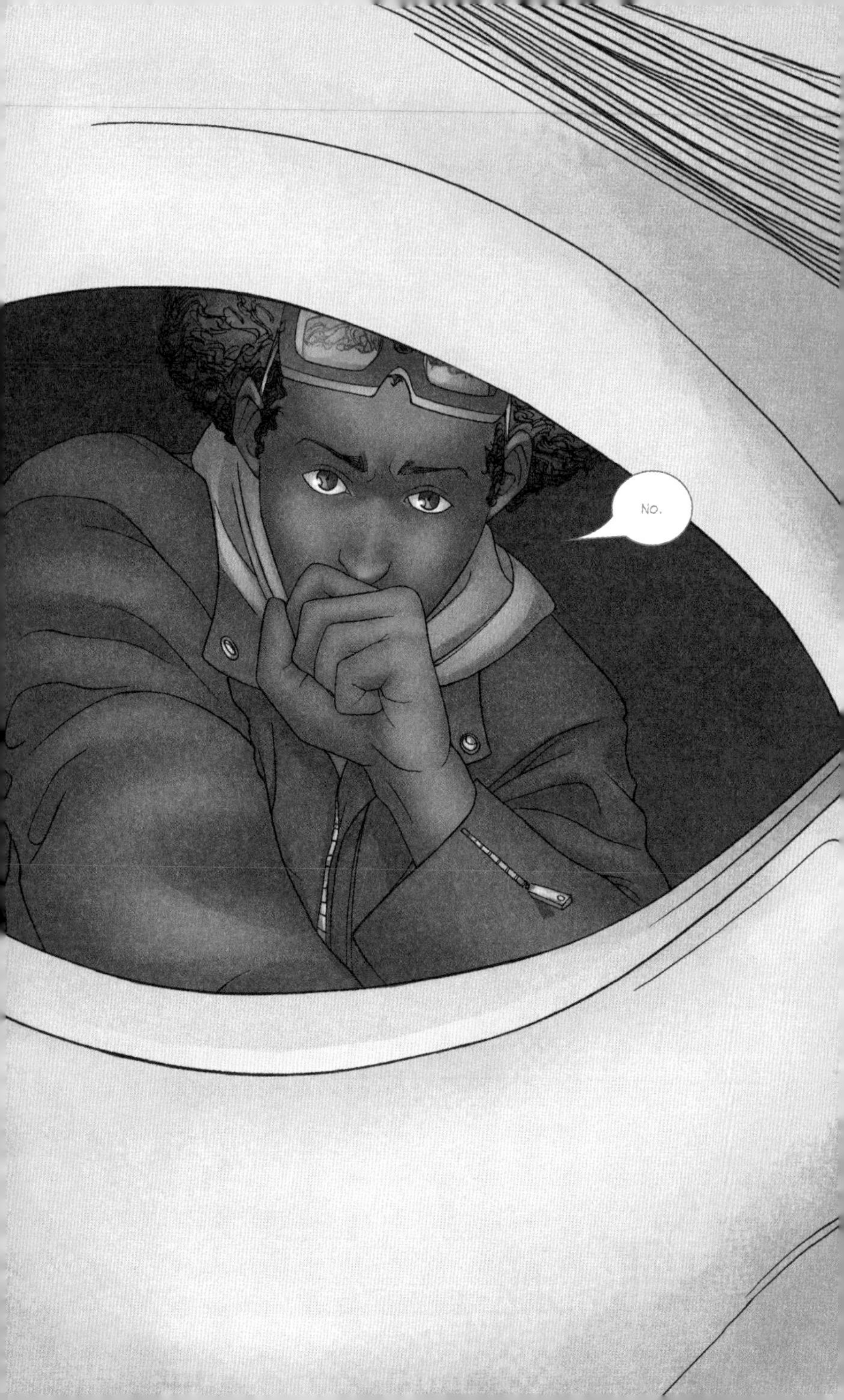
NO.

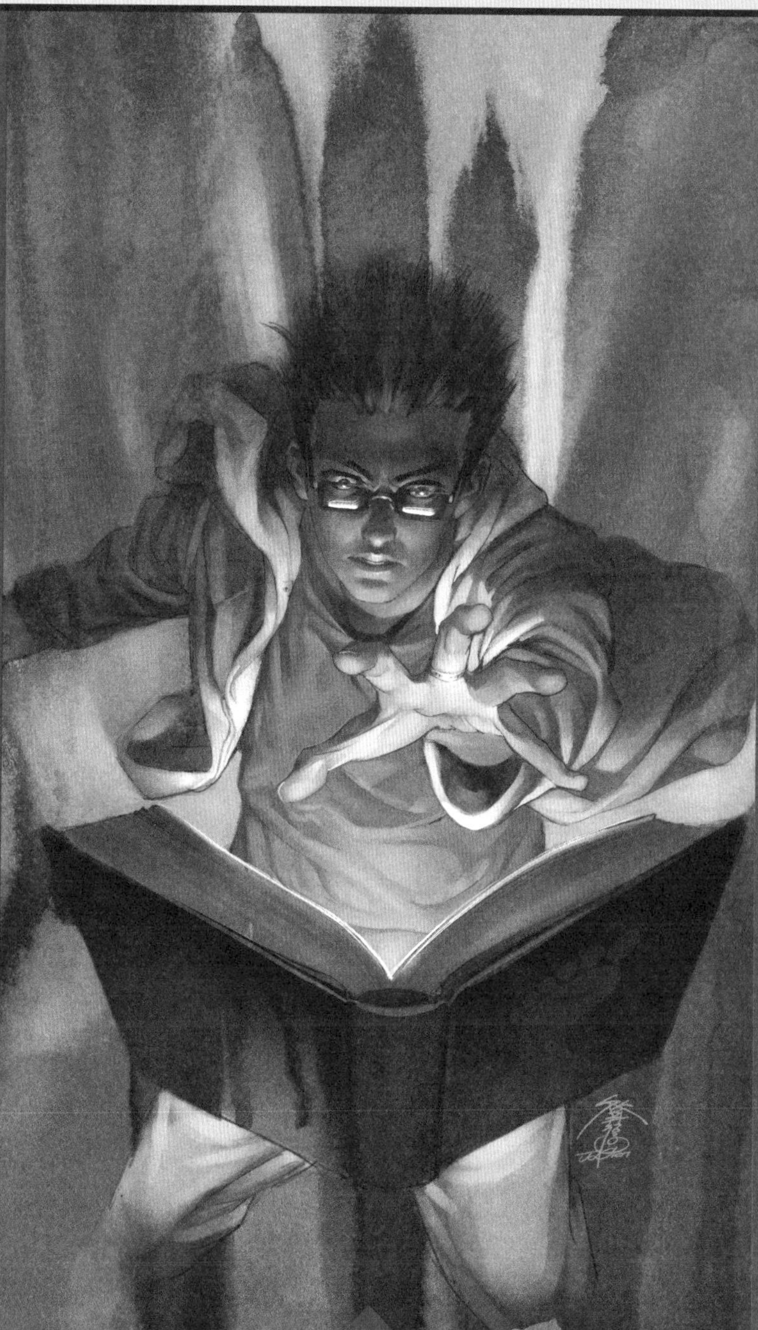
#9

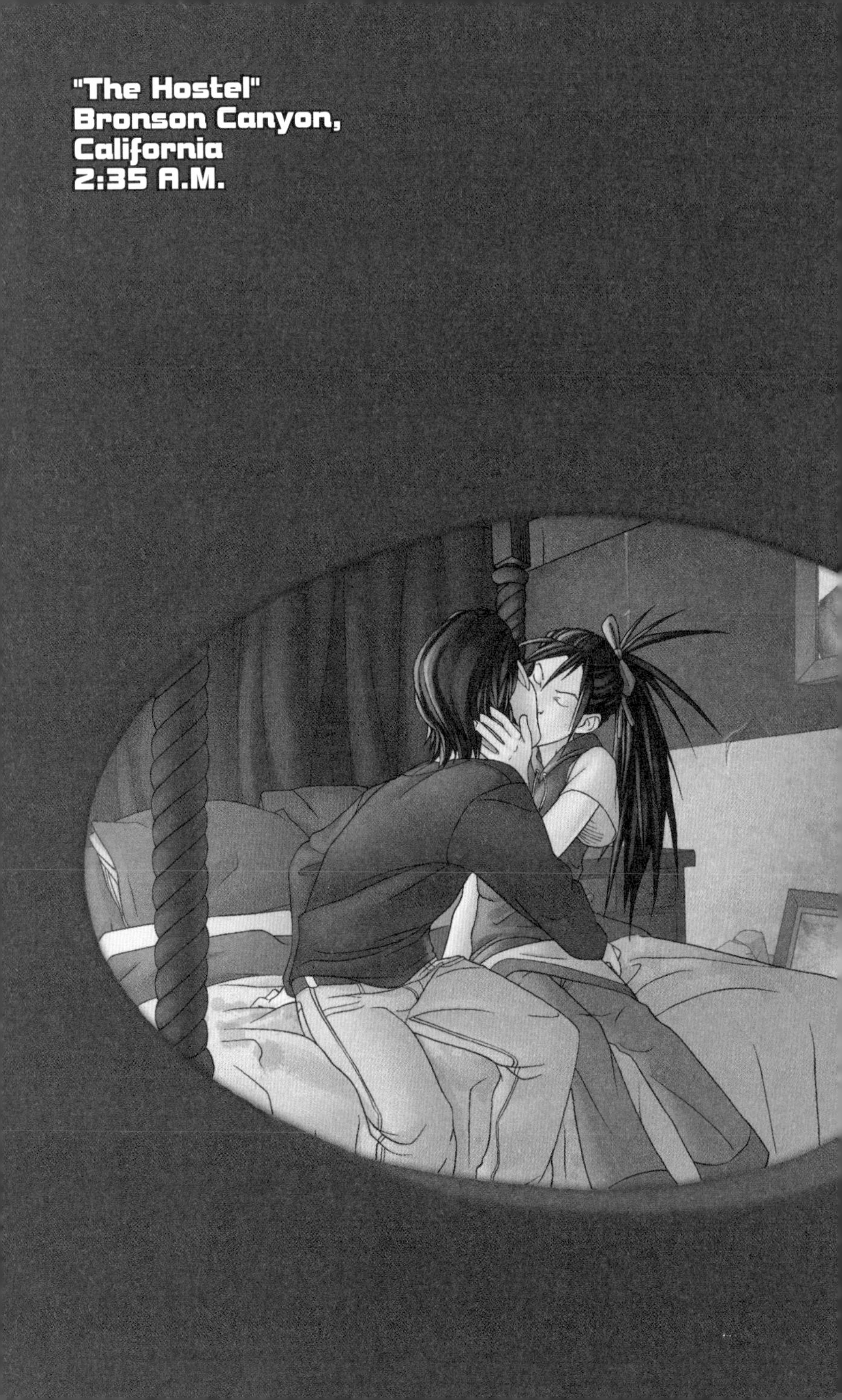
"The Hostel"
Bronson Canyon,
California
2:35 A.M.

DANGER
CATABA
TESTING SITE
LETHAL LEVELS OF
RADIATION

I don't know what to say, Alex.

You've been so sweet to me, and I've been acting like a total--

Nico...

No, you have to hear this. I just did something completely awful, and you deserve to--

Nico, I already know that you and Topher kissed.

You... you do? HOW?

Oh, our first night in the Hostel, I found this *secret room* next door. It's sorta like those passage-ways in my parents'--

You've been *spying* on me?

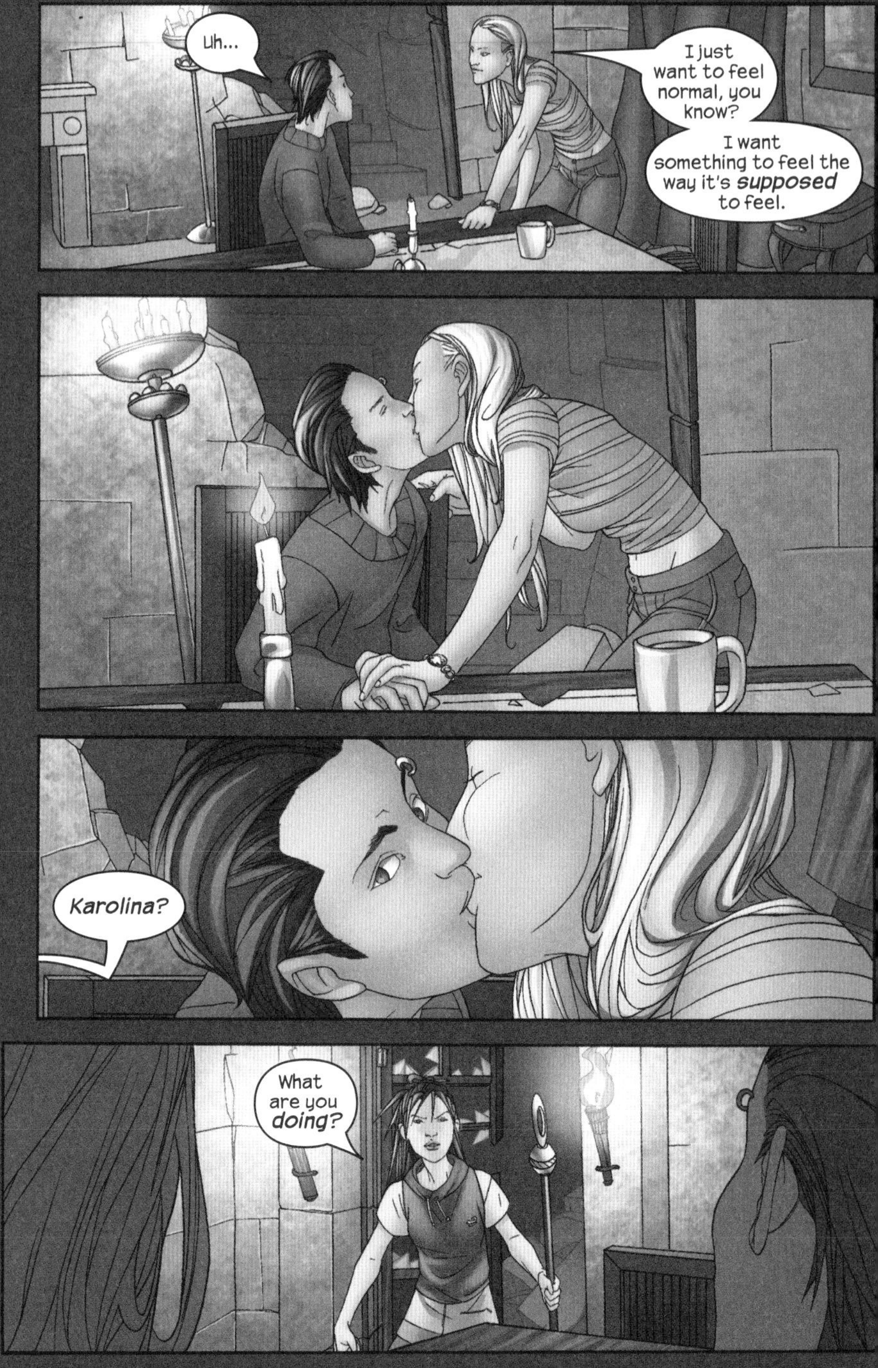
Uh...
I just want to feel normal, you know?
I want something to feel the way it's *supposed* to feel.
Karolina?
What are you *doing?*

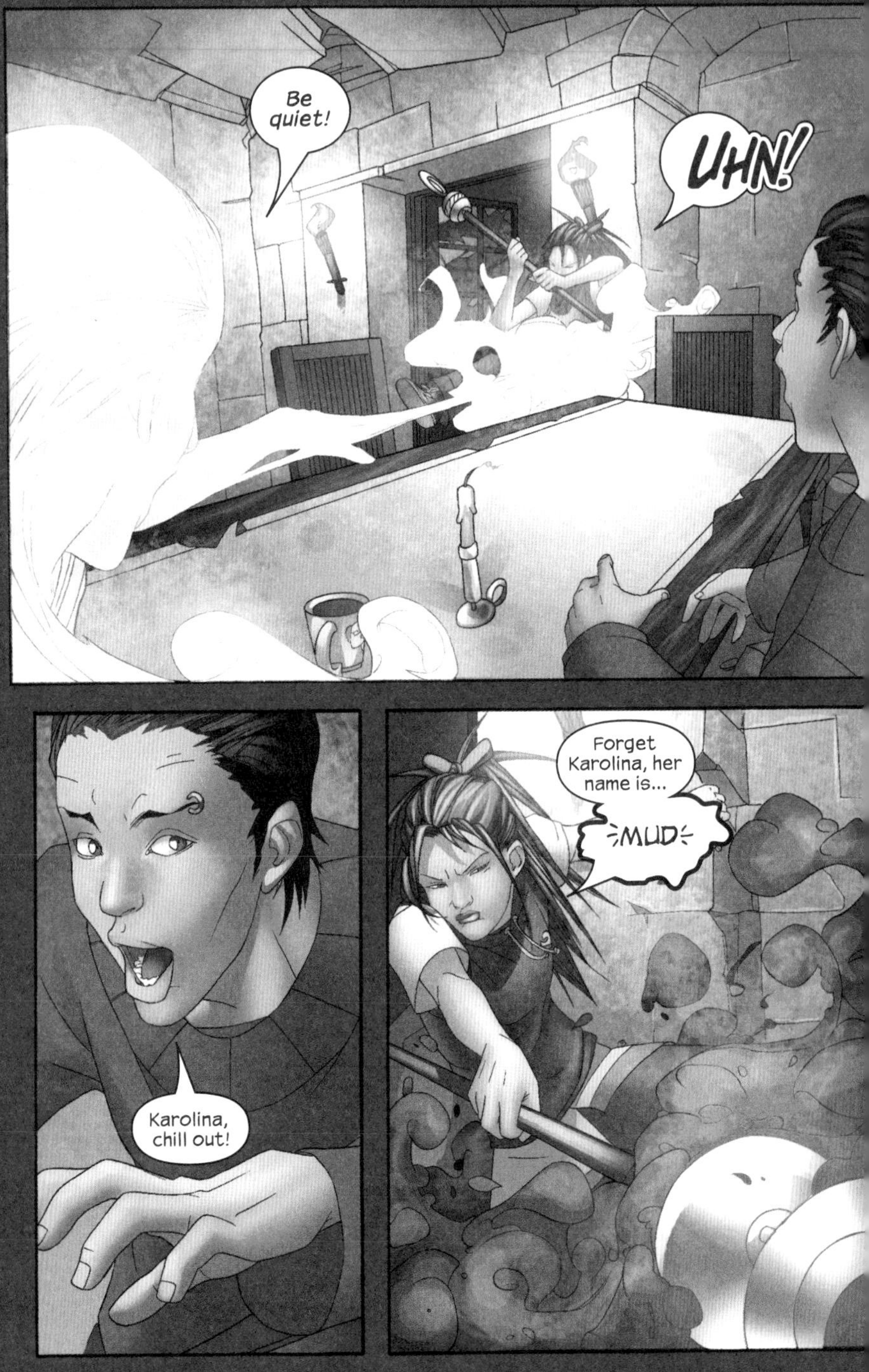
Be quiet!
UHN!
Karolina, chill out!
Forget Karolina, her name is...
MUD

"...set it free."

Any progress, dear?

Some. The rest of The Pride and I have been attempting to identify the three unregistered rogues who attacked our children.

So far, all we know is that at least two of the trio appear to possess augmented strength, speed, and some degree of invulnerability.

Well then, they're most likely *mutants*, no?

That's precisely what I was about to ask the good Dr. Hayes.

It's possible, Wilder, but not likely.

My pureblood union notwithstanding, it's extremely rare to encounter more than one mutant with the exact same power. These lowlifes probably just stumbled onto a cursed artifact or... or *radioactive meteorite*. You know, the usual.

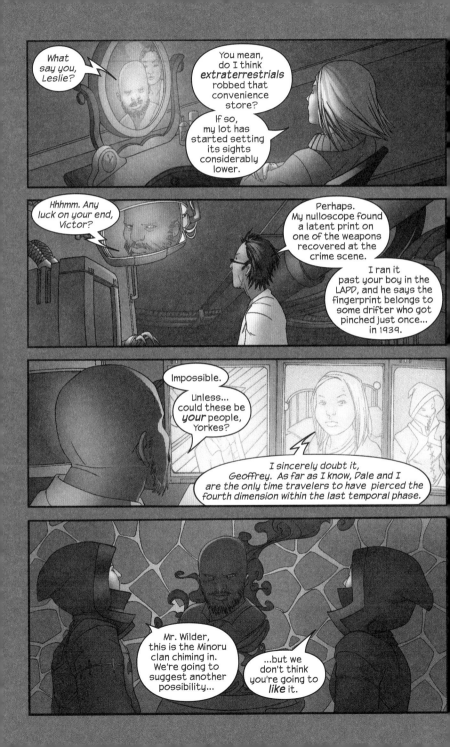

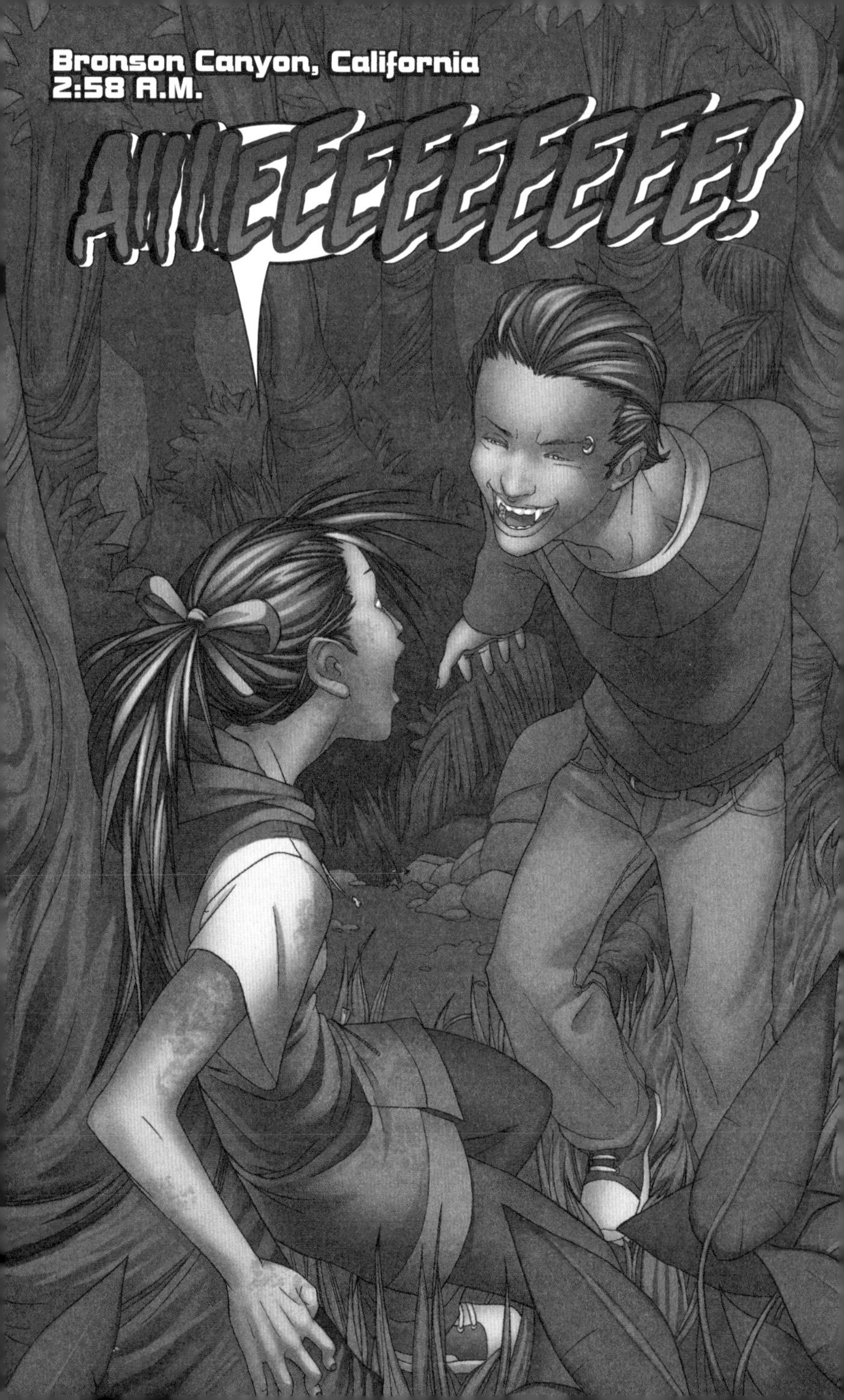
Bronson Canyon, California
2:58 A.M.
AIIIEEEEEEEEEEE!

You're lying. You have some kind of... of *hypnotic stare.* That's why we've all been acting so strange around you.
No, you've been acting so strange because you're *teenagers.* You're stupid, predictable, and easy to manipulate.
But *you,* you at least have *spunk.* That's why I'm going to *turn* you... and let you help me kill your *friends.*
No...
Too bad that scary magic wand is still trapped inside your perky little chest, huh? How are you going to *stop* me?
More importantly, why would you *want* to? I mean, I can give you *immortality.*
Besides, it doesn't look like you spend much time in the *sun* as is.
I... I don't want to be *evil.*
Becoming a vampire doesn't change who you are.
Growing up does that, letting the naiveté of adolescence be washed away by the cold hard water of life.
Trust me, when you've seen as much of *"humanity"* in action as I have, you start to realize that we're all just a bunch of animals.
And that means it's eat... or be eaten.

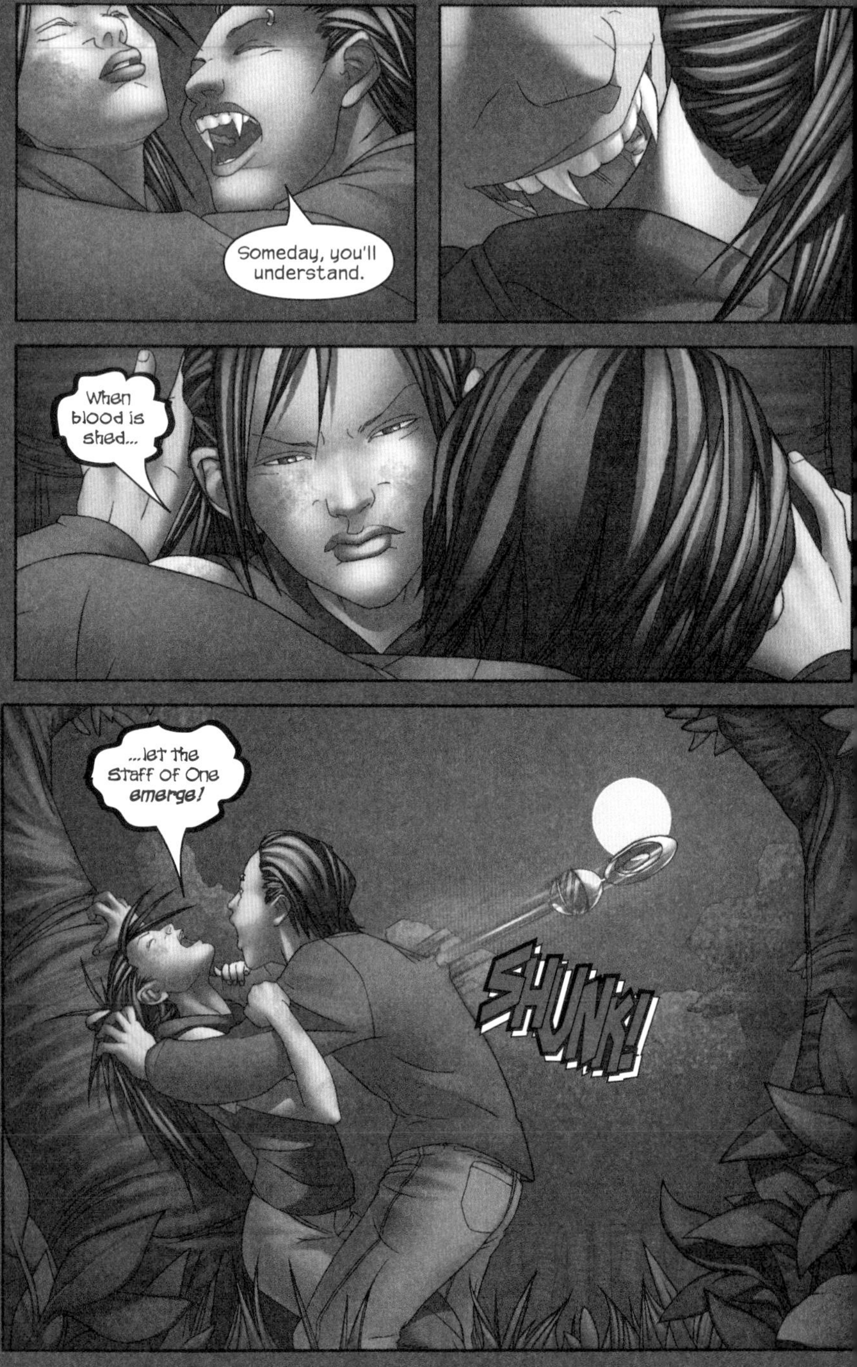

Someday, you'll understand.
When blood is shed...
...let the Staff of One emerge!
SHUNK!

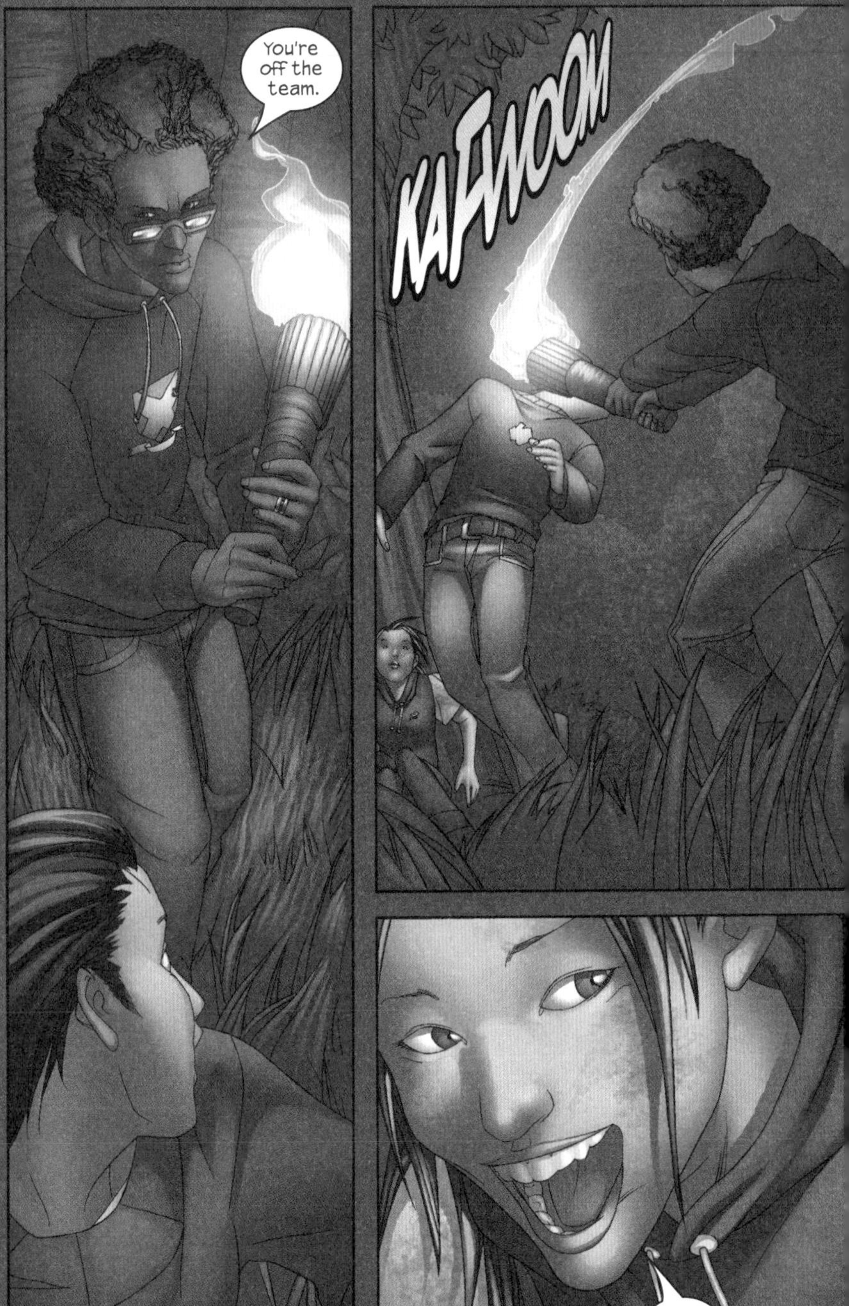
You're off the team.
KAFWOOM
Alex!

I'm sorry, I... I came looking for you because I was *jealous,* and I know it was wrong but I--

I love you!

I love you, too. Can you walk?

No, I can *run.* Come on!

Hurry! He heals fast!

So Topher's a... a *vampire?* Vampires are *real?*

Unless we're all having the exact same *nightmare...*

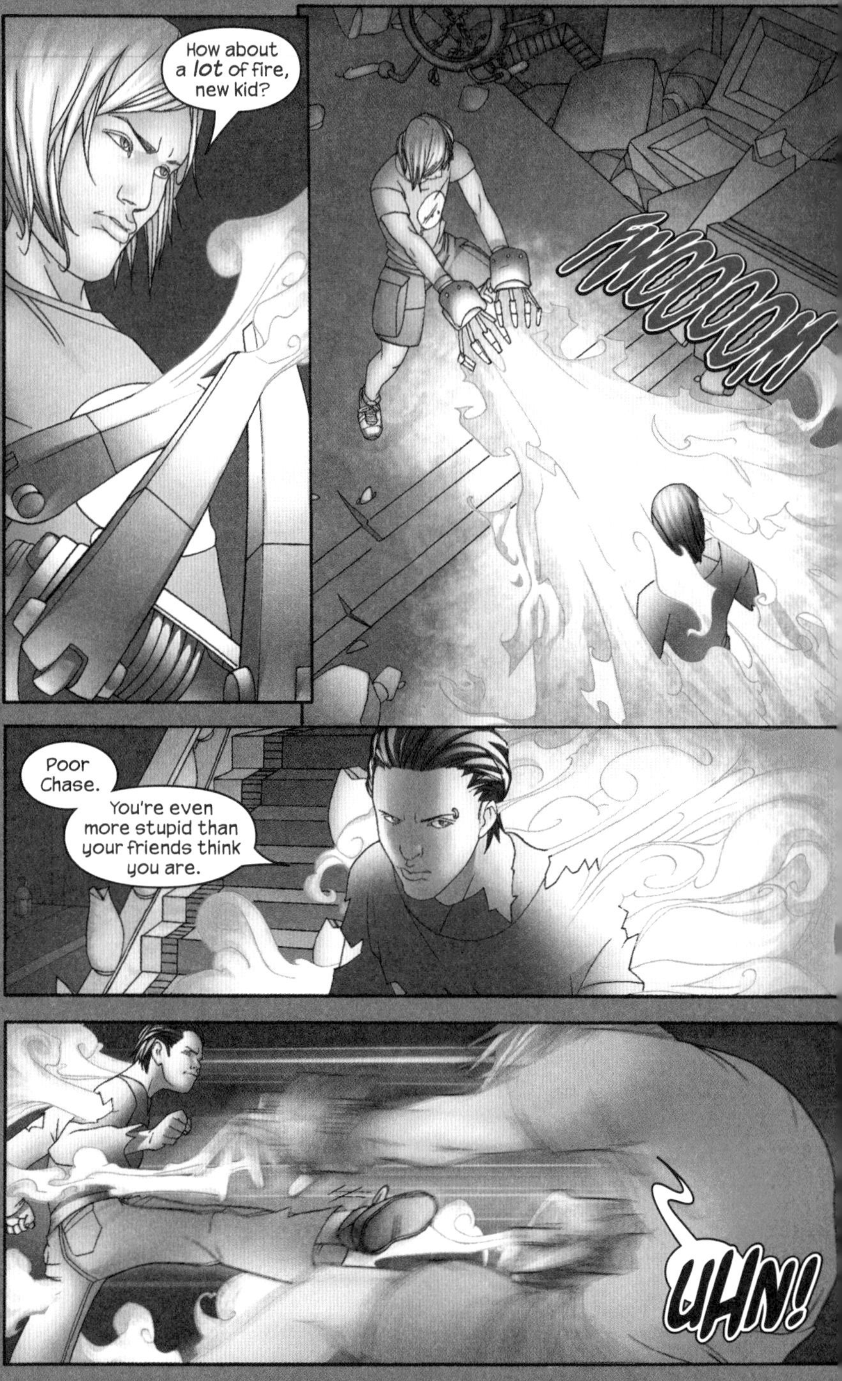

How about a *lot* of fire, new kid?
FWOOOOOM
Poor Chase.
You're even more stupid than your friends think you are.
UHN!

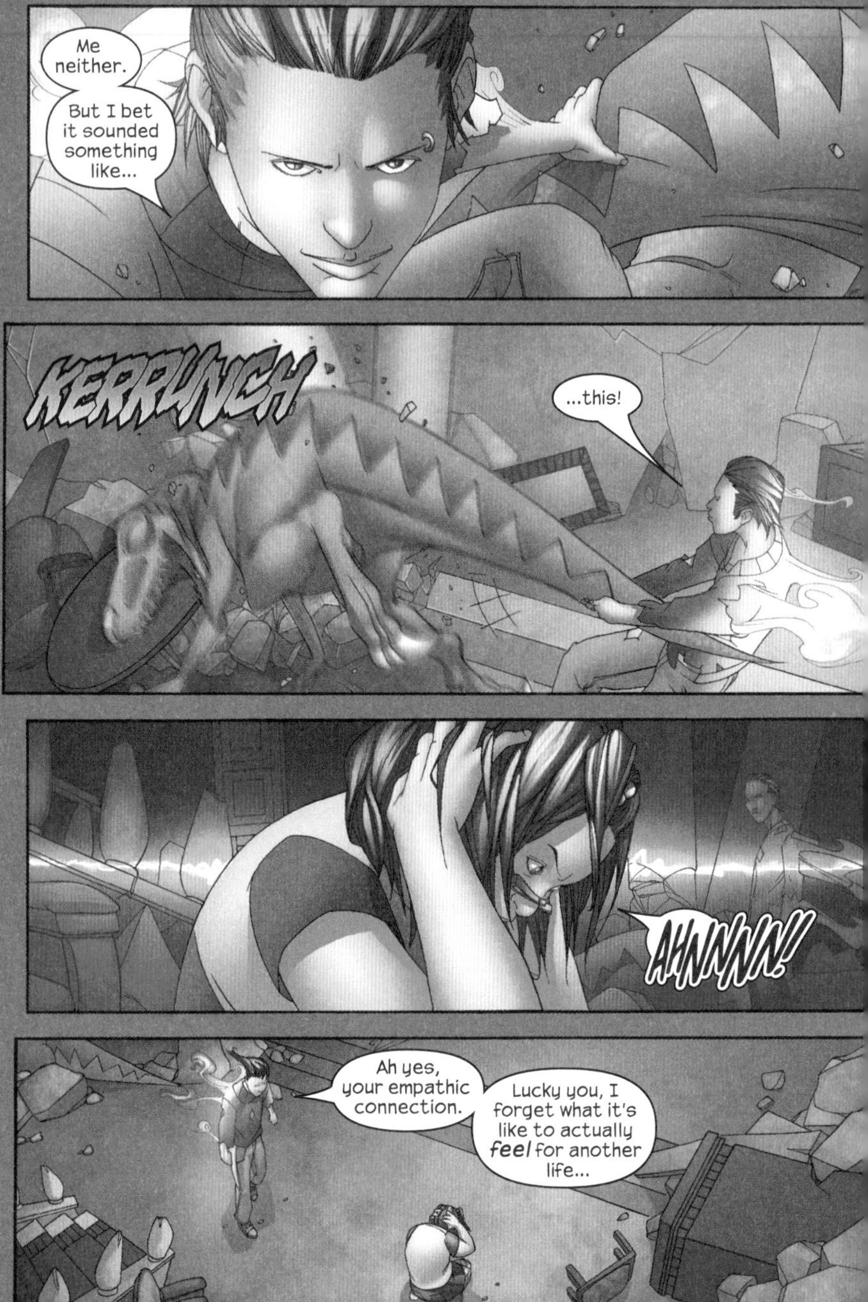
Me neither.
But I bet it sounded something like...
KERRUNCH
...this!
AHNNNN!
Ah yes, your empathic connection.
Lucky you, I forget what it's like to actually *feel* for another life...

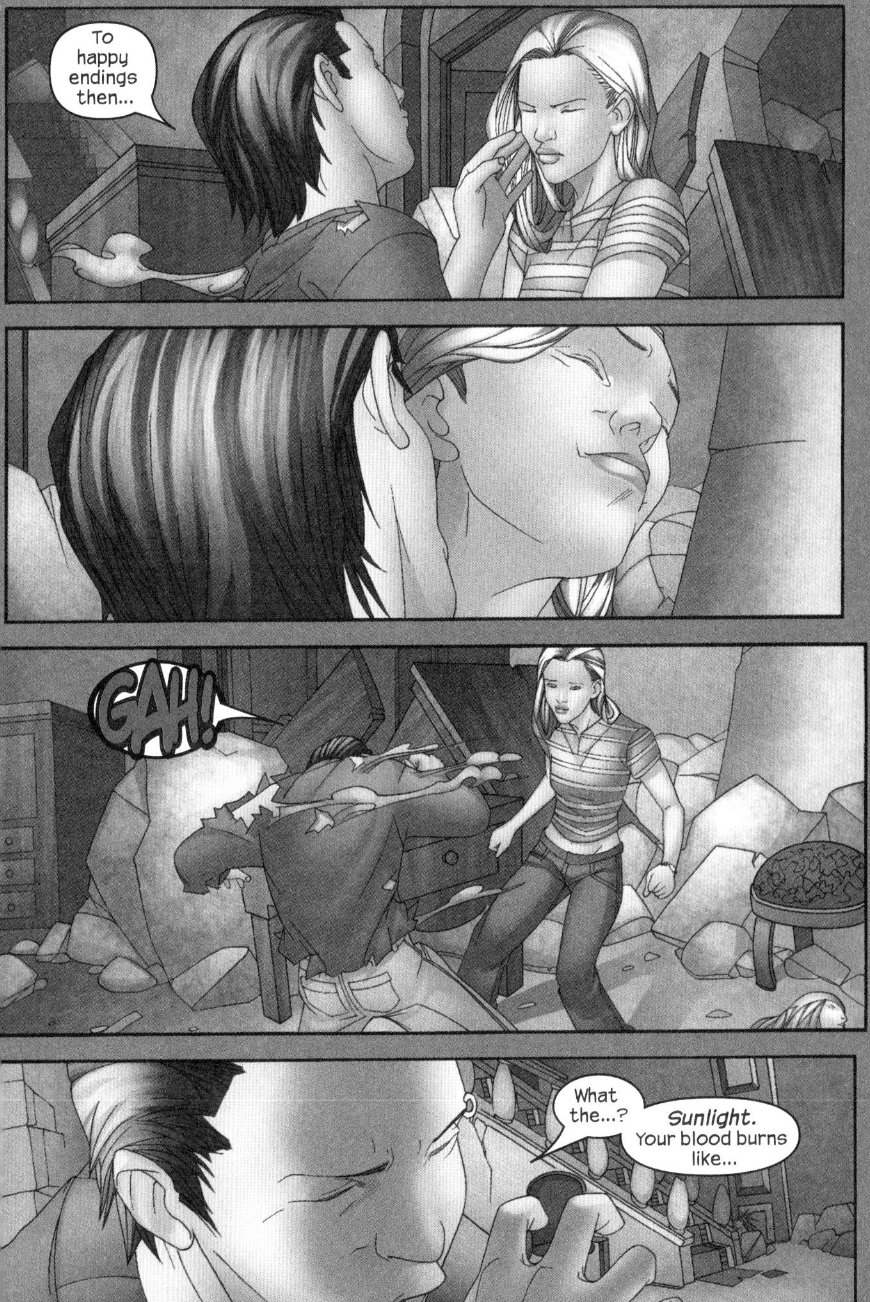
To happy endings then...
GAH!
What the...?
Sunlight. Your blood burns like...

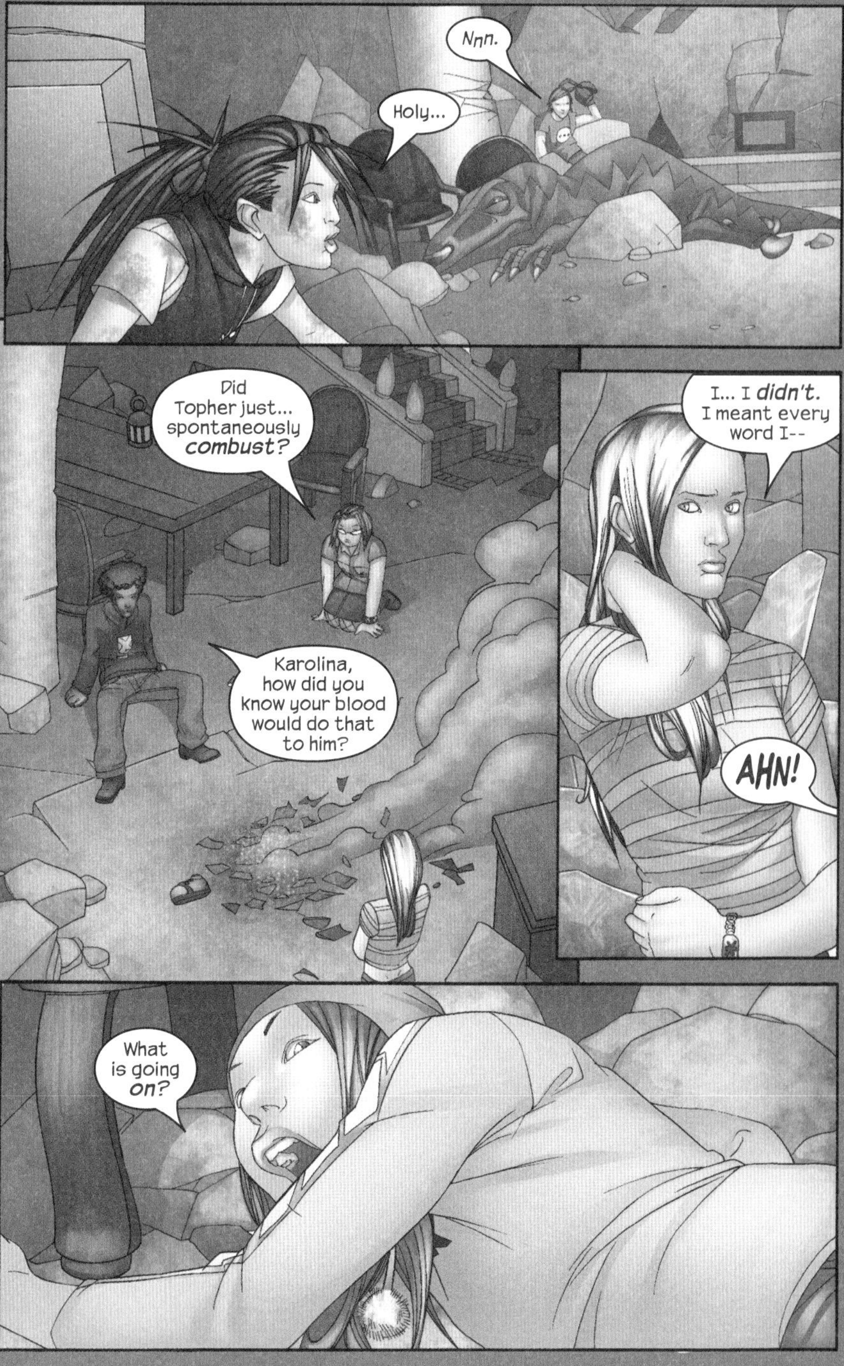
Nnn.
Holy...
Did Topher just... spontaneously *combust?*
Karolina, how did you know your blood would do that to him?
I... I *didn't.* I meant every word I--
AHN!
What is going *on?*

#11

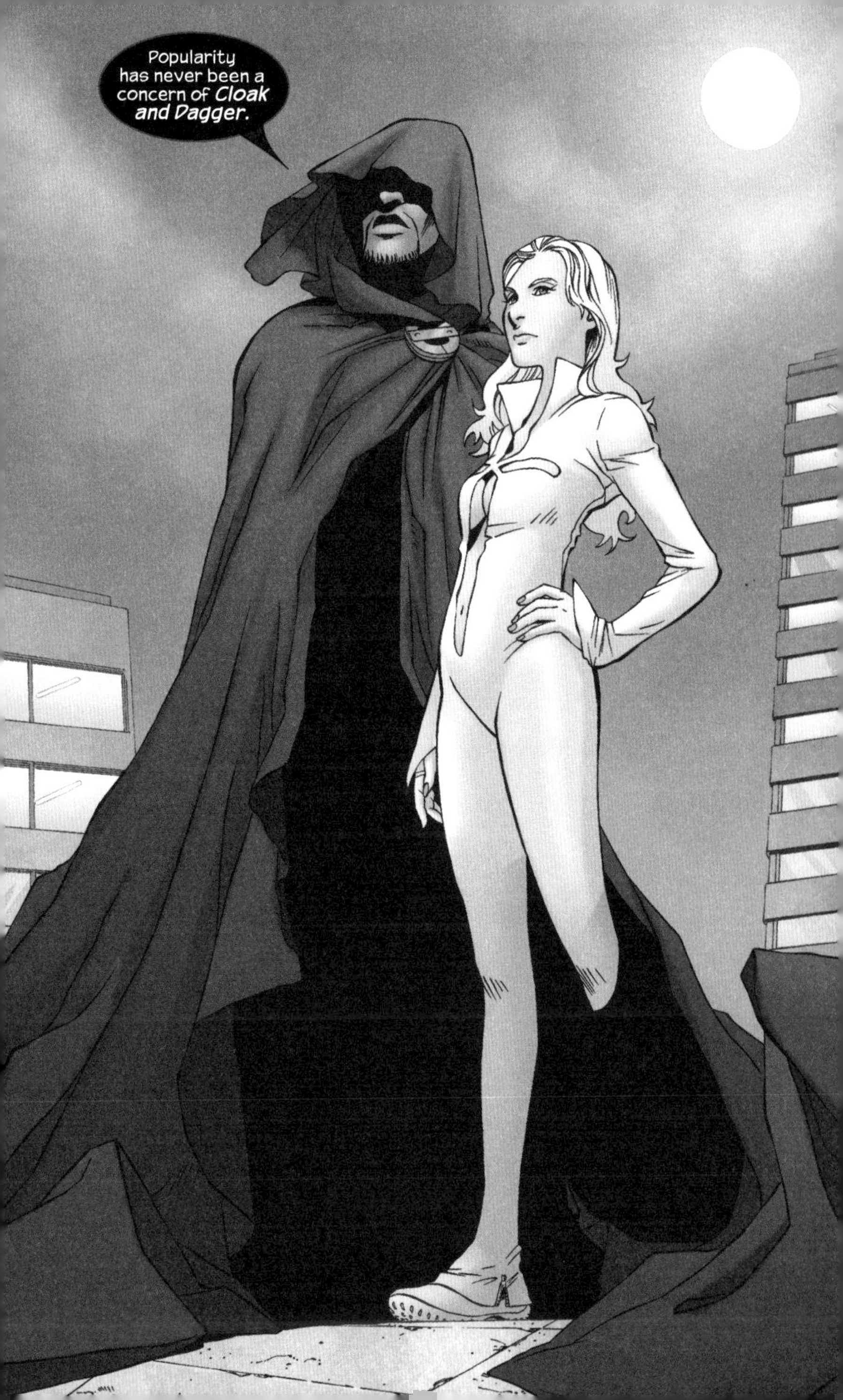
Popularity has never been a concern of *Cloak and Dagger*.

But don't confuse us with the *junkies* you deal with every night, Lieutenant Flores.

The experimental pharmaceuticals that gave us our powers over light and darkness were *forced* on us by evil men...

...lowlifes who preyed on the fact that me and Cloak were helpless little runaways.

Since that day, Dagger and I have vowed to help *all* children in need.

Swell, 'cause we could sure use a hand finding a few *runaways* of our own.

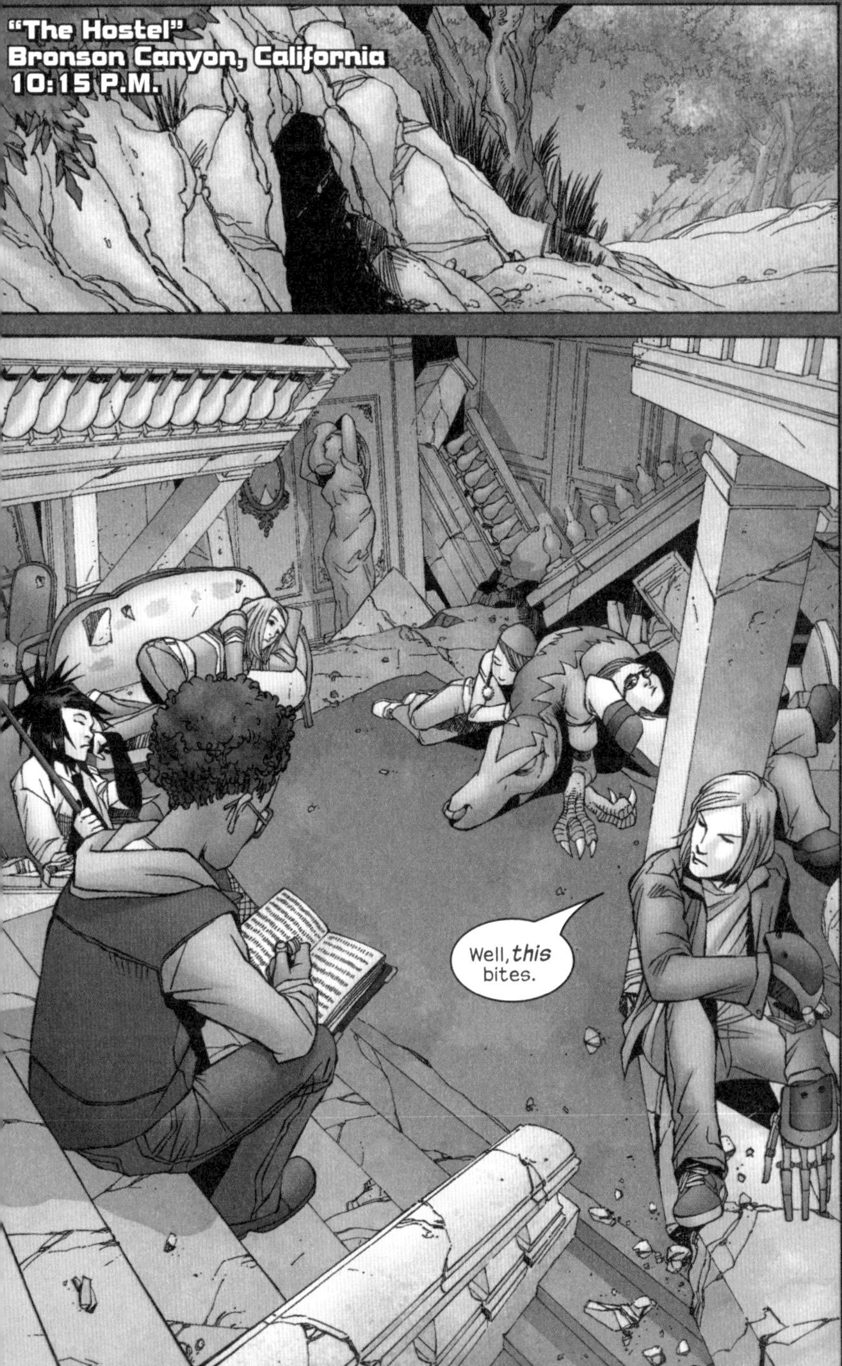
"The Hostel"
Bronson Canyon, California
10:15 P.M.
Well, *this* bites.

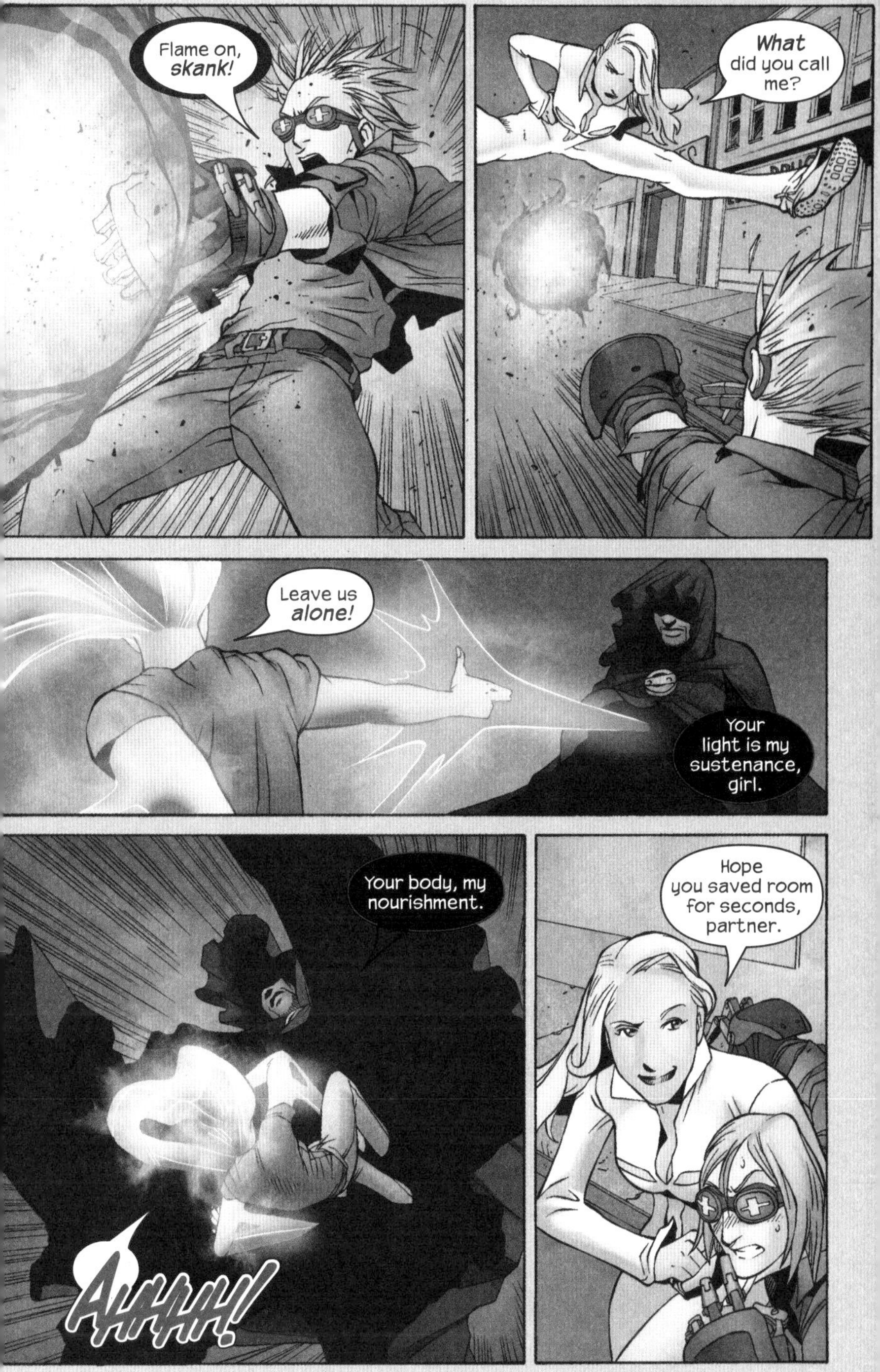
Flame on, *skank!*
What did you call me?
Leave us *alone!*
Your light is my sustenance, girl.
Your body, my nourishment.
AHHHH!
Hope you saved room for seconds, partner.

Nice.

We didn't take down *Stilt Man* that fast.

Hn.

Uh-oh, I don't like the sound of *that* grunt.

My relationship with the Darkforce Dimension has been... *temperamental* since my original abilities were restored during our misadventure in *Cleveland*.

Still, the four within my cloak's shadowy realm... I sense no stain of *blood* on their souls.

What are you saying? They're *not* murderers?

It is possible.

And yet, in one of them, I do recognize a powerful *darkness*, a--

Hey, Desdemona!

What the--?

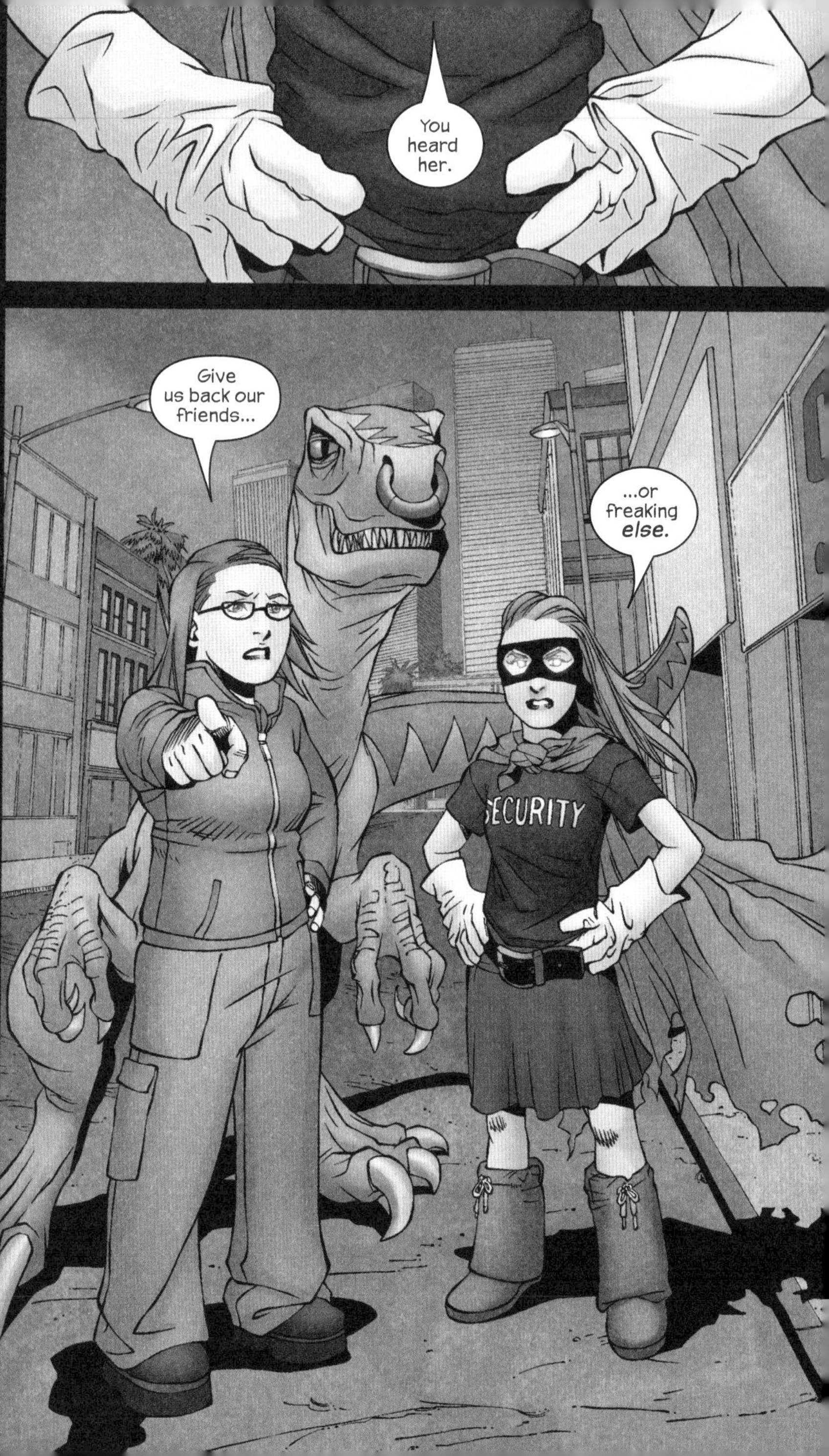
You heard her.
Give us back our friends...
...or freaking *else.*

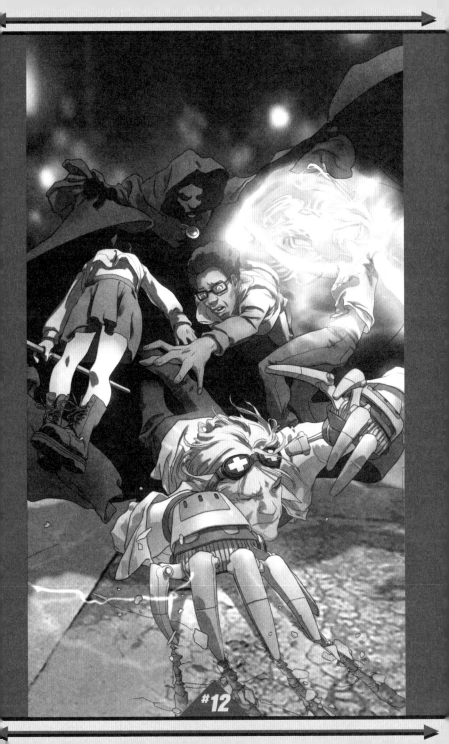

#12

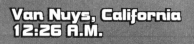

Huh.

You know, it says a lot about my life that this *isn't* the strangest thing I've ever seen.

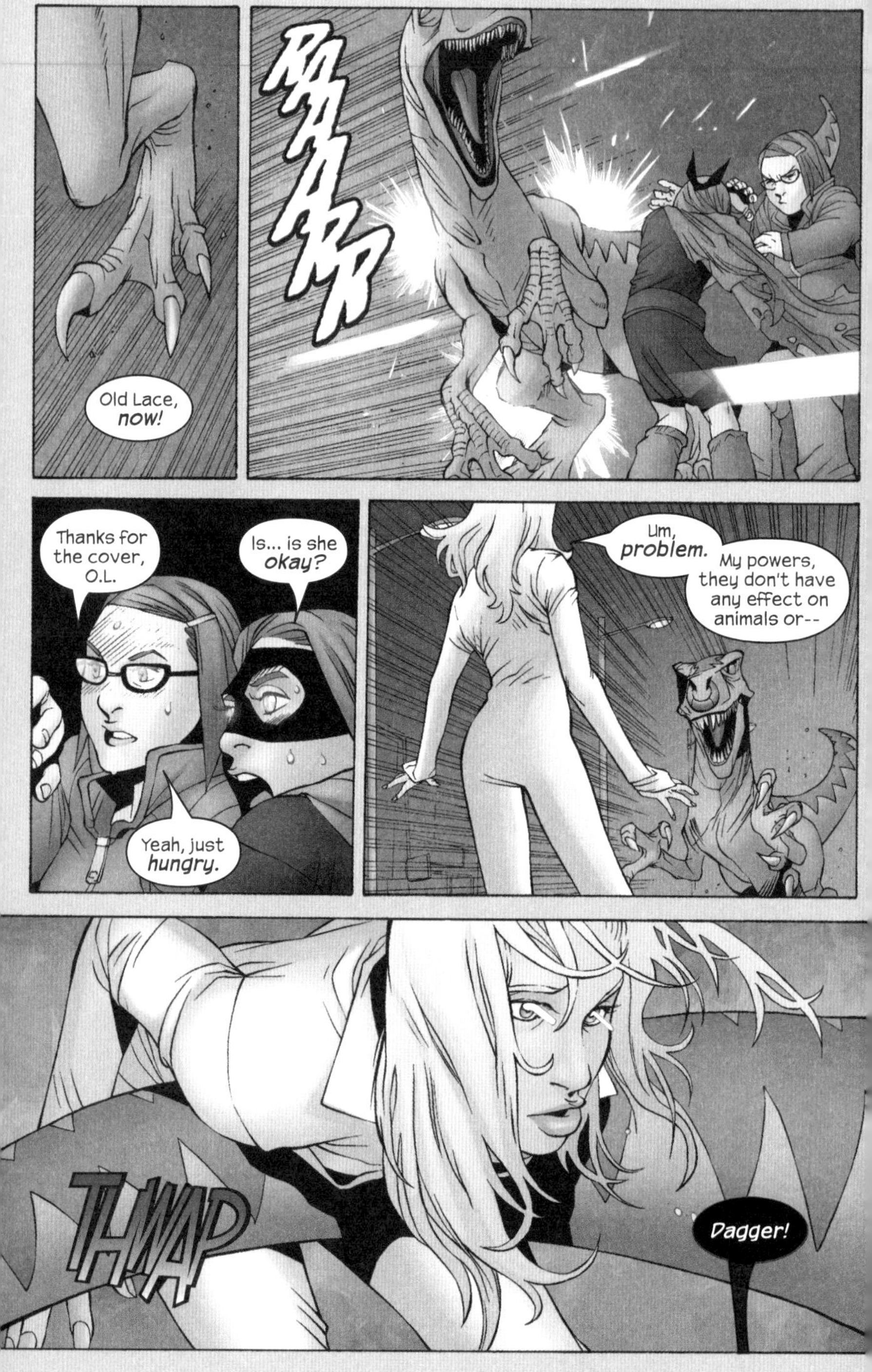
Old Lace, *now!*
RRAAARRR
Thanks for the cover, O.L.
Is... is she *okay?*
Yeah, just *hungry.*
Um, *problem.*
My powers, they don't have any effect on animals or--
THWAP
Dagger!

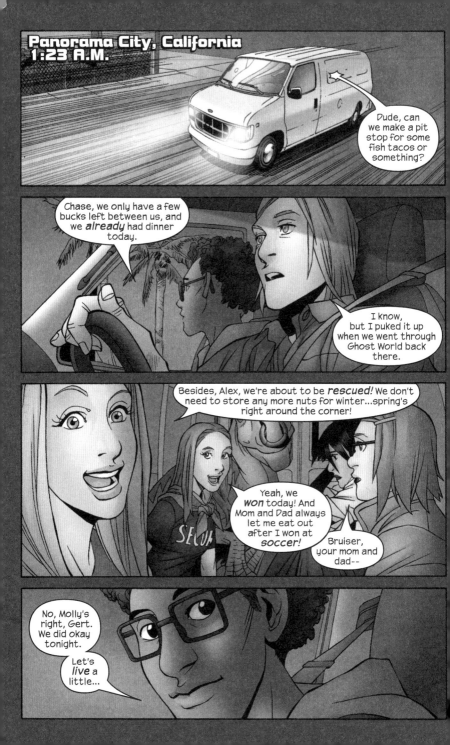

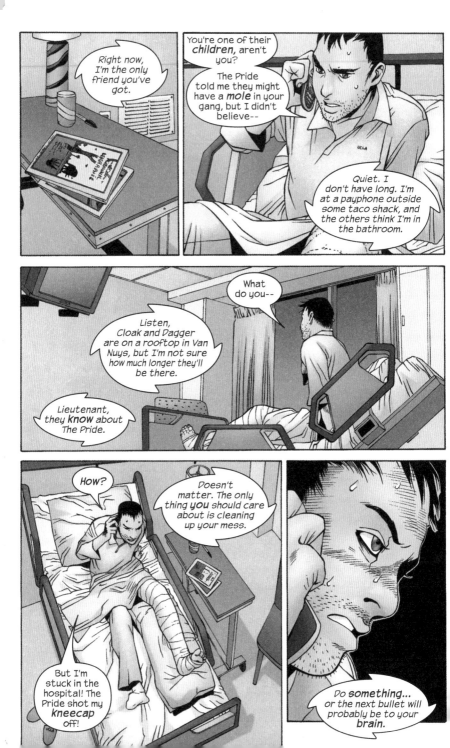

LA MEDIC

Are you strong enough for the journey home now, Tandy?

I am if you are.

I feel terrible for dragging you out here. I was easily duped by the kind of authority you and I used to always *question.*

Don't beat yourself up, Ty. We both made mistakes...

...but maybe something *good* will come from--

KASCHOWW!

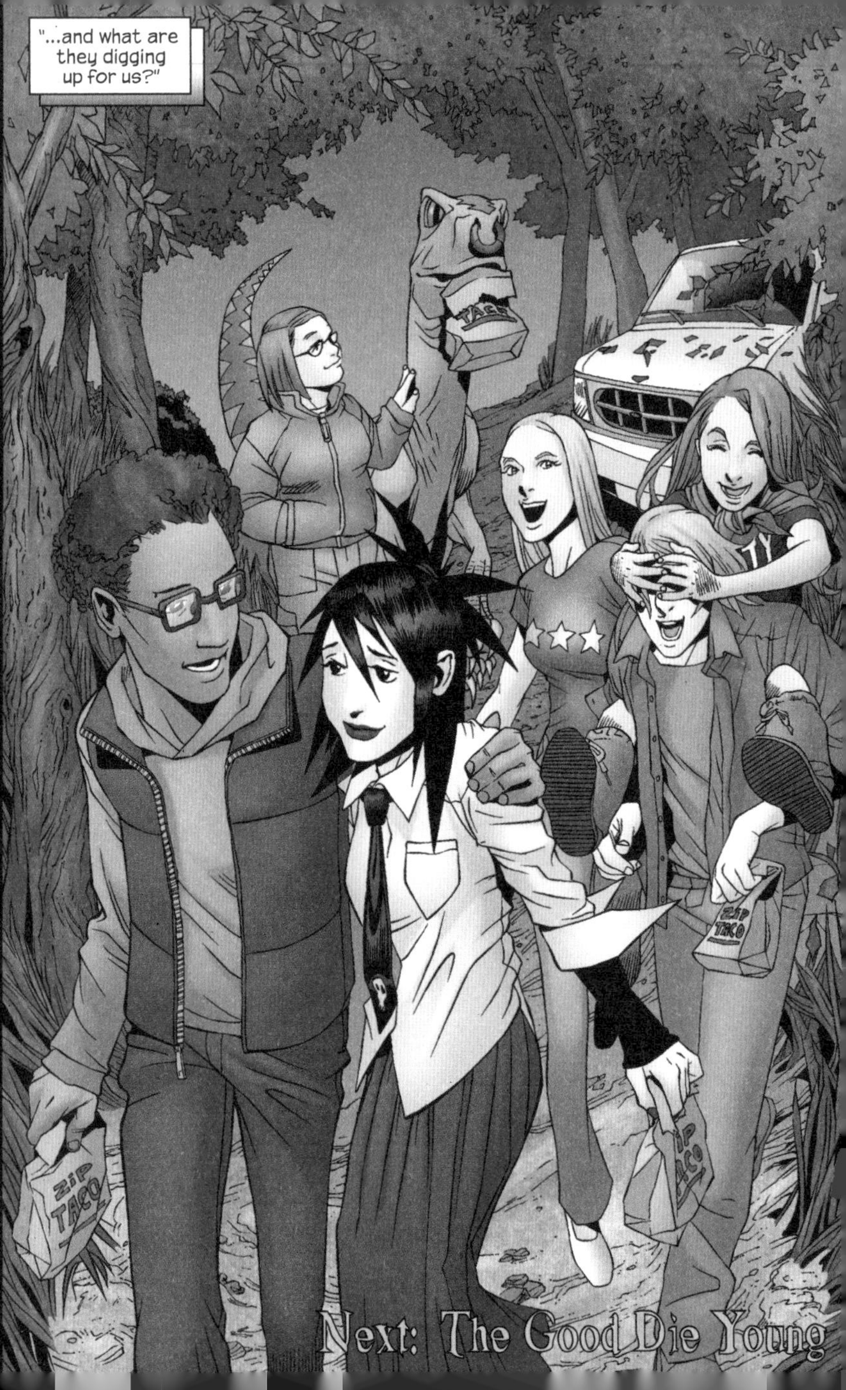
"...and what are they digging up for us?"
TACO
TY
ZIP TACO
ZIP TACO
ZIP TACO
Next: The Good Die Young